Jeanette Milde

Once Upon a Wedding

and

R&S
BOOKS

request the honor of your presence

....

at the marriage of

Anna Glad and Alfredo Felice

in the Little Church in the Woods
Dinner and dance will follow

R&S
BOOKS

Stockholm   New York   London   Adelaide   Toronto

The bride was beautiful in the dress of her dreams.

The groom polished both his shoes and his dance steps one last time.

Anna and Alfredo wanted lots of little flower girls and ring bearers in their wedding. Little angels with rosy cheeks and sparkling smiles—just the kind of children they themselves hoped to have someday. But does anything ever turn out the way you plan?

Agnes was the flower girl.

"I don't want to be the flower girl!
I want to be the bride."
"But, Agnes, don't you think that would
make the bride feel sad? Brides are so
sensitive on their special day."
"Well, if she has to be the bride, then
I want to be a fairy."
"But, Agnes . . ."

John and Paul were the ring bearers.

John had just made an important discovery and did not have time for a wedding. And Paul just couldn't hold still.

The wedding could begin. Well, almost.
All their family and friends were sitting
patiently in the pews.
Nobody knew what was keeping the bride
and groom.

"I have a loose tooth," whispered John.
"When it falls out, I'm going to put it under
my pillow. And then I'll get a present—from
the tooth fairy."
"I know," said Agnes.
"But the tooth has to be fresh," John added.
"What do you mean, 'fresh'?" asked Agnes.

"There has to be fresh blood on it," answered John.
"BLOOD! Do you think you'll lose your tooth today?"

"I will," said the groom.
"I will," said the bride.
"I will," said John.
"Cool!" Agnes thought.

"How are you going to get it out?" Agnes wondered.
"Maybe with a piece of string," said John. "I'll tie it to a truck. And then—

VROOM!

Bye-bye, tooth!"

Suddenly everybody started smooching and hugging and—worst of all—pinching cheeks.

OUCH! I'm a fairy.

My little angel, just look how you've grown!

"Do you have any string?" Agnes asked.
"Nope," said John.

"This is weird food," said John.
"But if we don't eat it, we'll hurt the bride's feelings.
Brides are so sensitive on their special day."
"We'll say it in a nice way," said John.

"Boy, is it noisy in here!"
"Yeah, I can't even hear what I'm eating.
Let's get out of here!"

"We'll pretend we're in the African jungle."
"I can see your underpants," said John.
"They're red and black."
"Wrong," said Agnes.
"Can I see them again, then?"

"They're my rose panties," said Agnes.
"Cool! Do you want to see mine?" John asked.
"Okay."
"But I'm not wearing my very best ones today."
"Well, I think they're pretty nice," said Agnes.
"Thanks!" said John.

GROWL!

"Let's play that the shoes are really angry space cats that want to yank out your tooth."
"Okay, but let's say we tamed them and put them in a circus," said John.

"You want to get married?" asked Agnes.
"Would you kiss me then?"
"Would I have to?"
"I think so."
"Naw, let's just pull out your tooth instead."
Agnes borrowed someone's shoelace.

OUCH!

"Come on! Don't you want a present from the tooth fairy?"
"Yeah, but . . . Let's go look at the wedding presents first."

"Let's say you choose first, and then show me what you got," said Agnes.

"What do you wish for from the tooth fairy?" asked Agnes.
"A coin maybe. Or some candy. Or a little tiny toy."

"Look, a cake! Do you think it's your present from the tooth fairy?"
"My tooth hasn't fallen out yet, but anyway I think we get to taste it."

"They sure are noisy over there," said John.
"It's the jungle people trying to get at your tooth," said Agnes. "Let's hide!"

"We'll hide under the table!"

"Look! My tooth is stuck in the apple!"
"You're bleeding. Great! The tooth is fresh.
 You can wish for something!"

Then someone got the bright idea of
looking under the table again.
And he could tell everyone:
Shh! Here are the little angels.

The bride's shoes were there as well. BINGO!
"Look, someone has lost a tooth.
We need to call the tooth fairy!"

The tooth fairy appeared in a twinkling.
She turned the tooth into a gold coin.

While John and Agnes slept, there was dancing and gladness and rejoicing.

Only one other guest had gotten just as tired.

And the bride and groom lived happily ever after. (Any little angels? Yes, with rosy cheeks, who were also visited by the tooth fairy.)

"Wath will you buy with the money?"
(What will you buy with the money?)
"A wonderful, secret thing."
"Thell me!" (Tell me!)
"Will you kiss me if I tell you?"